Fairies in Wonderland

An Interactive Coloring Adventure for All Ages

Illustrations and Text
by Marcos Chin

HARPER
DESIGN

An Imprint of HarperCollinsPublishers

There are five gifts waiting for you in Wonderland. Find them by locating the correct number of magical lettered keys that are hidden within the five groups of drawings on the following pages. Collect all the keys and unscramble the letters to solve the riddle to collect the gift that will help you on the next leg of your journey.

It's time to put on your fairy wings...

start your coloring journey...and find magical things.

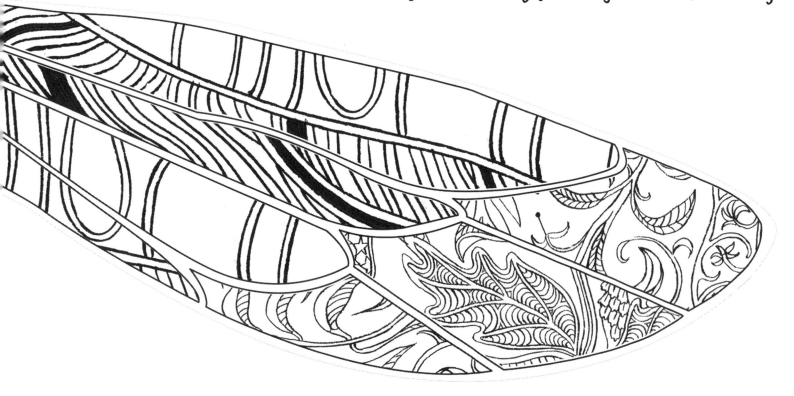

Find four keys in
this group of drawings
to answer the riddle
on page 23.

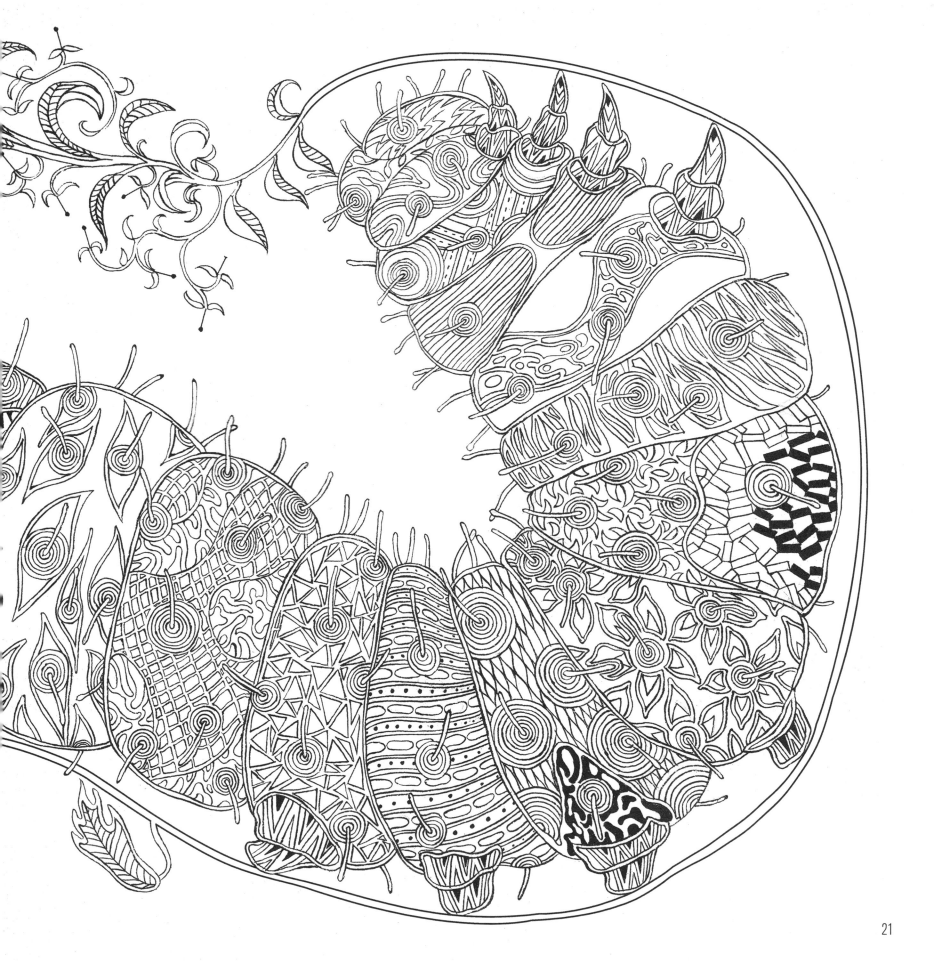

With the feet of a duck
You will swim like a fish,
When you don these shoes
In the watery abyss.

What am I?

The letters of the four keys hold the answer.

Wear these FINS to help you swim
in the Wonderland sea and find ten
keys to answer the riddle on page 41.

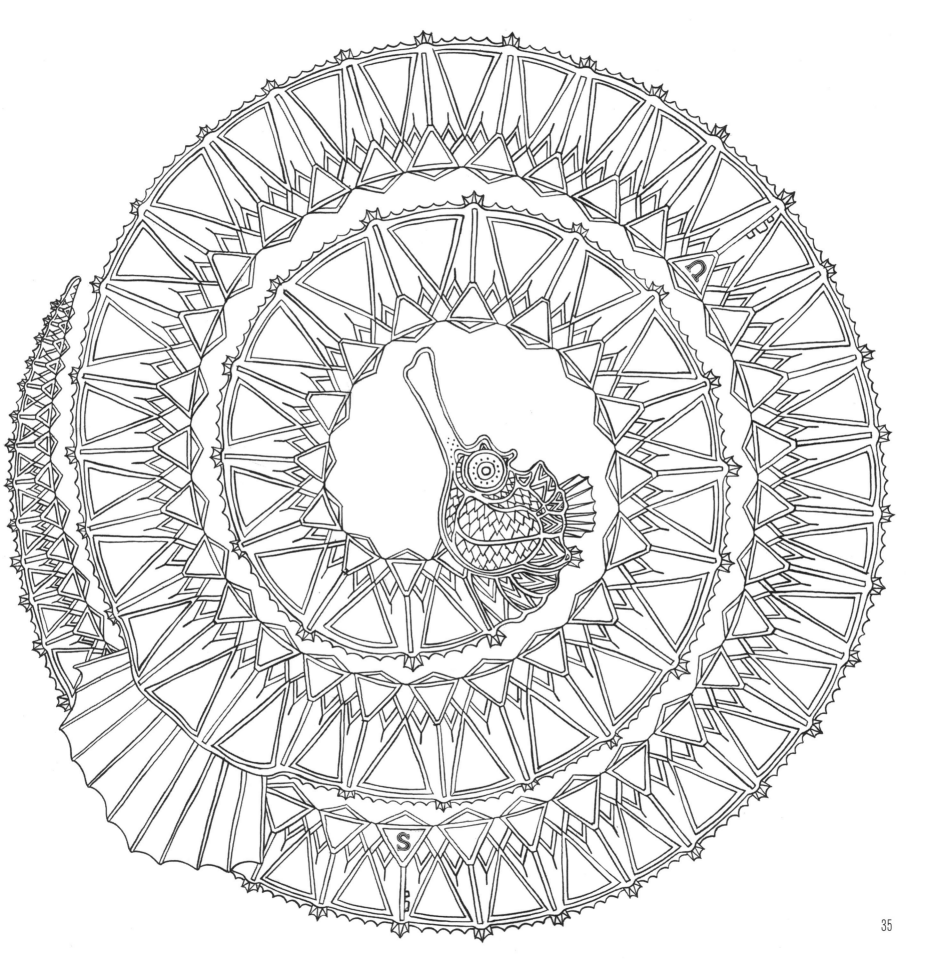

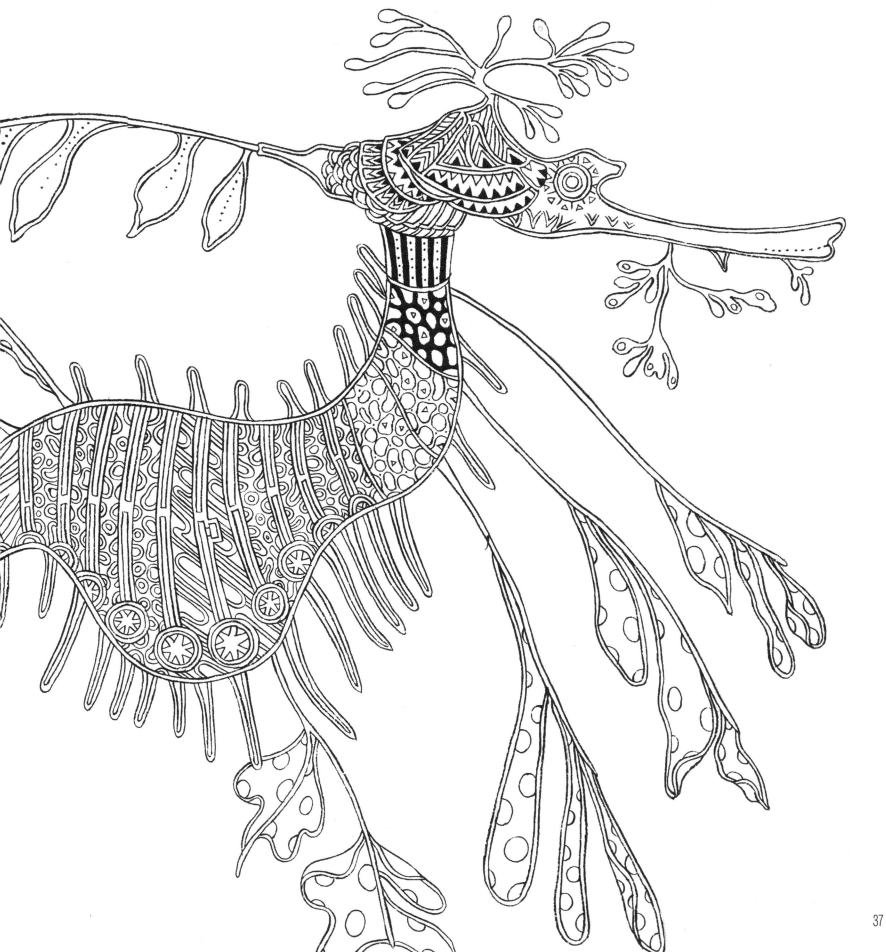

I am made of glass
But you can't drink from me.
Look through my darkness
So you can much better see.

What am I?

The letters of the ten keys hold the answer.

Wear these SUNGLASSES so you can fly high in the sunny Wonderland sky and easily spy the seven keys that form the answer to the riddle on page 57.

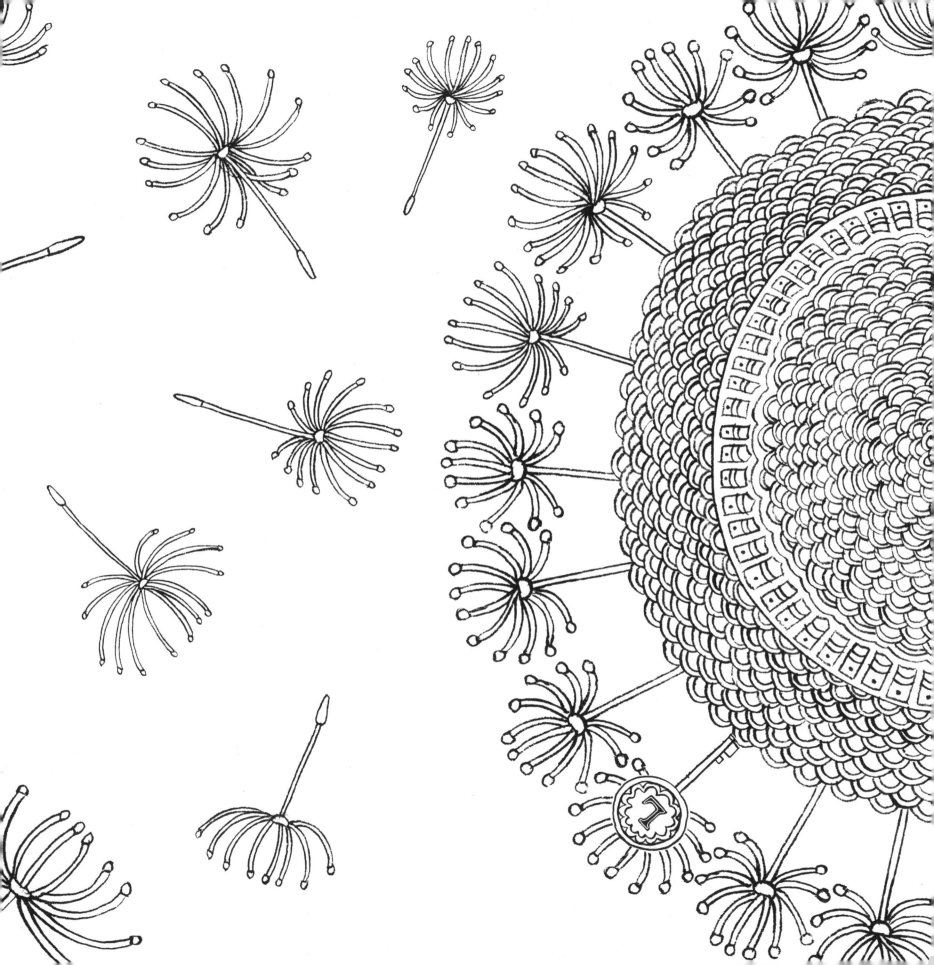

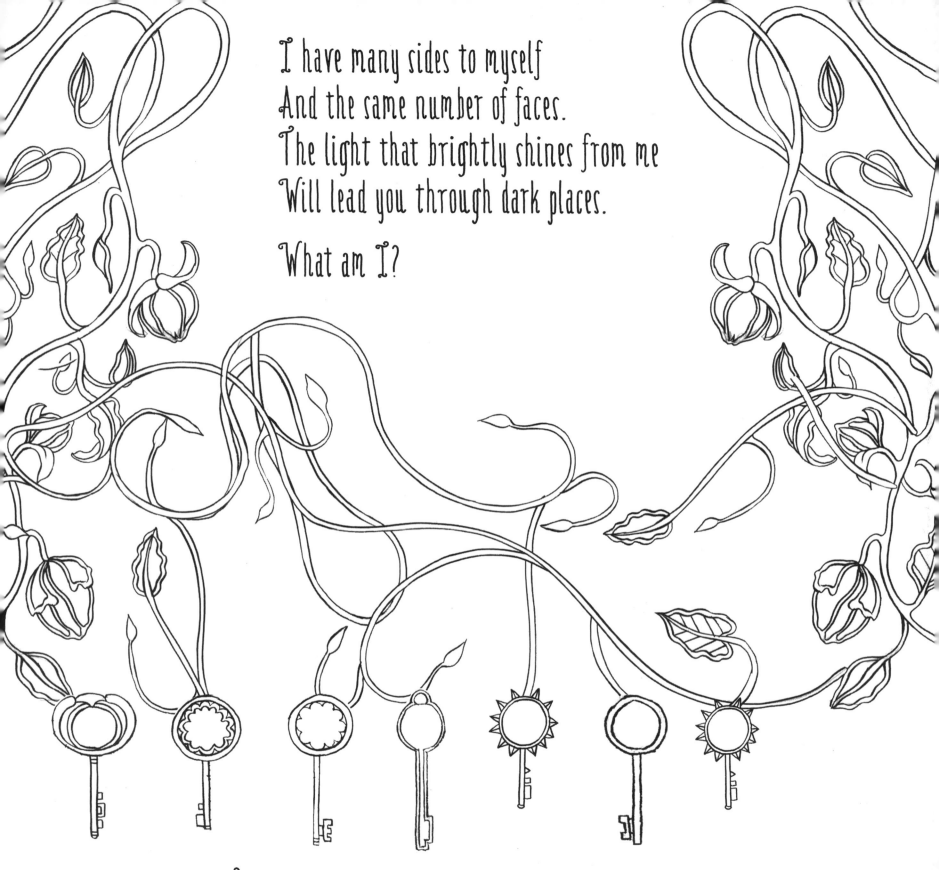

I have many sides to myself
And the same number of faces.
The light that brightly shines from me
Will lead you through dark places.

What am I?

The letters of the seven keys hold the answer.

Use the CRYSTAL to light your path at night in the Wonderland woods and to find the five keys that form the answer to the riddle on page 75.

Blow air across my holes
And night creatures will sleep.
Hearing my woodwind songs,
They will not even peep.

What am I?

The letters of the five keys hold the answer.

Playing this magic FLUTE
will put unruly night creatures to sleep
and guarantee you safe passage through
the night as you search for six new keys
that form the answer
to the riddle
on page 91.

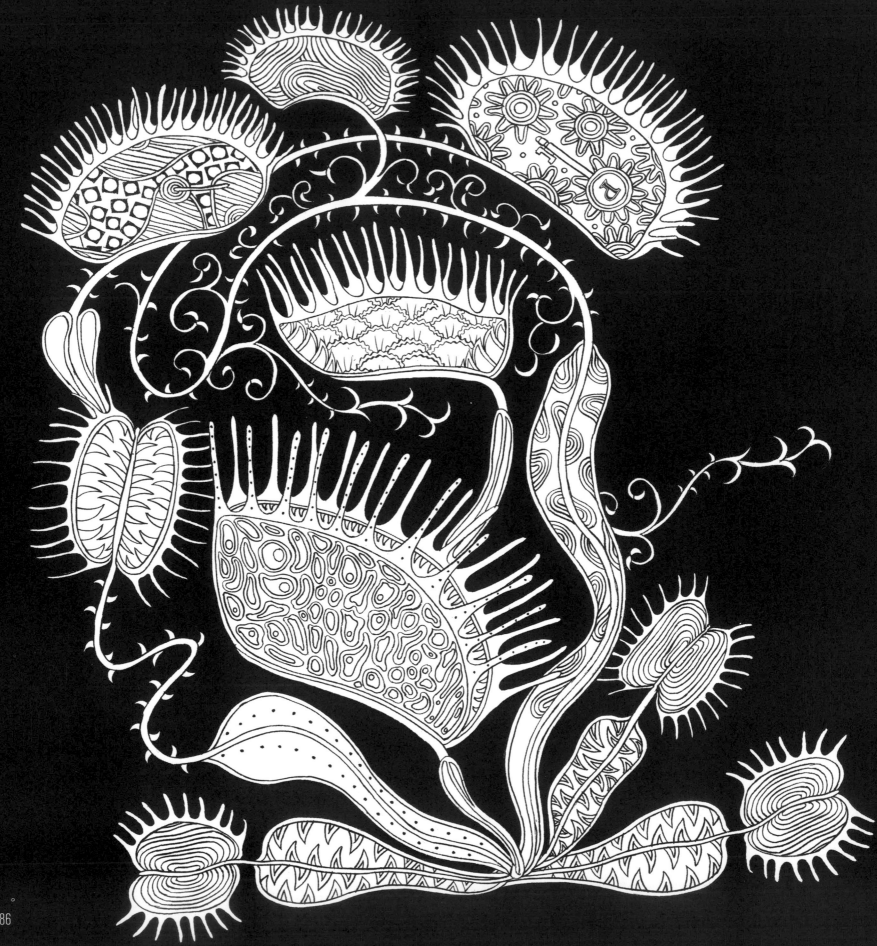

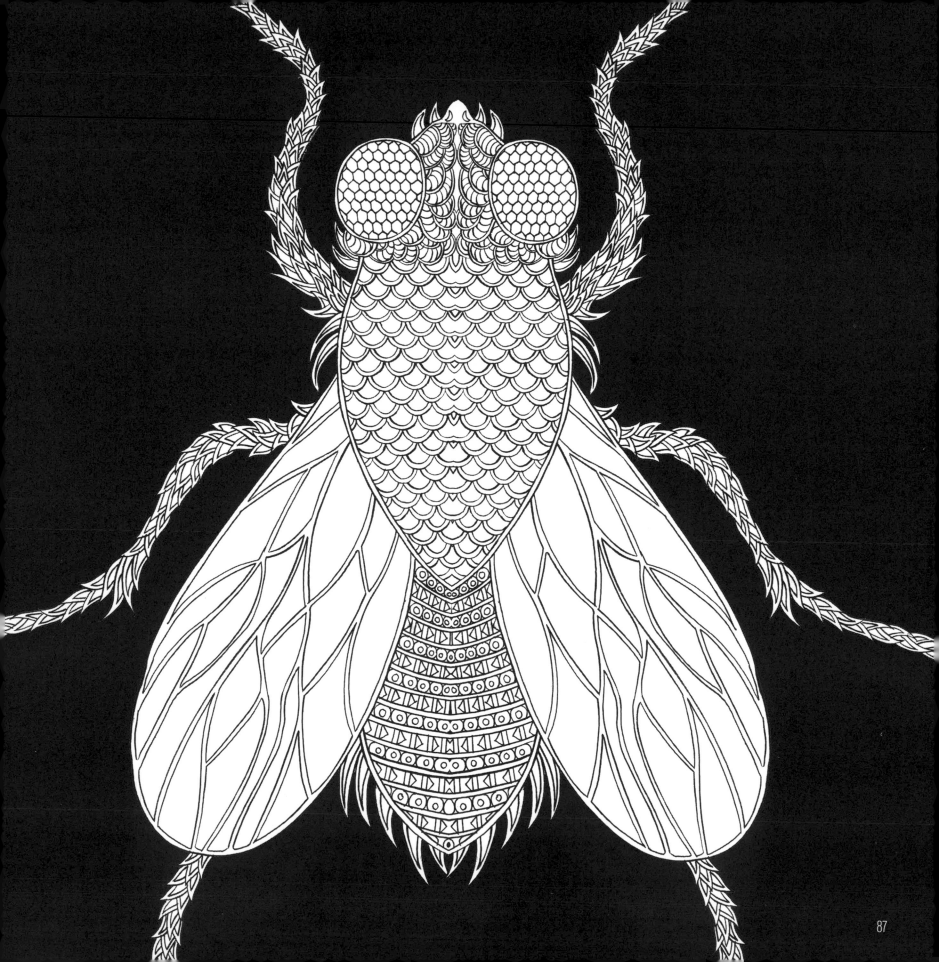

I give voice to those who use me
And grow shorter over time.
The marks I leave on the pulp of trees
Can be erased line by line.

What am I?

The letters of the six keys hold the answer.

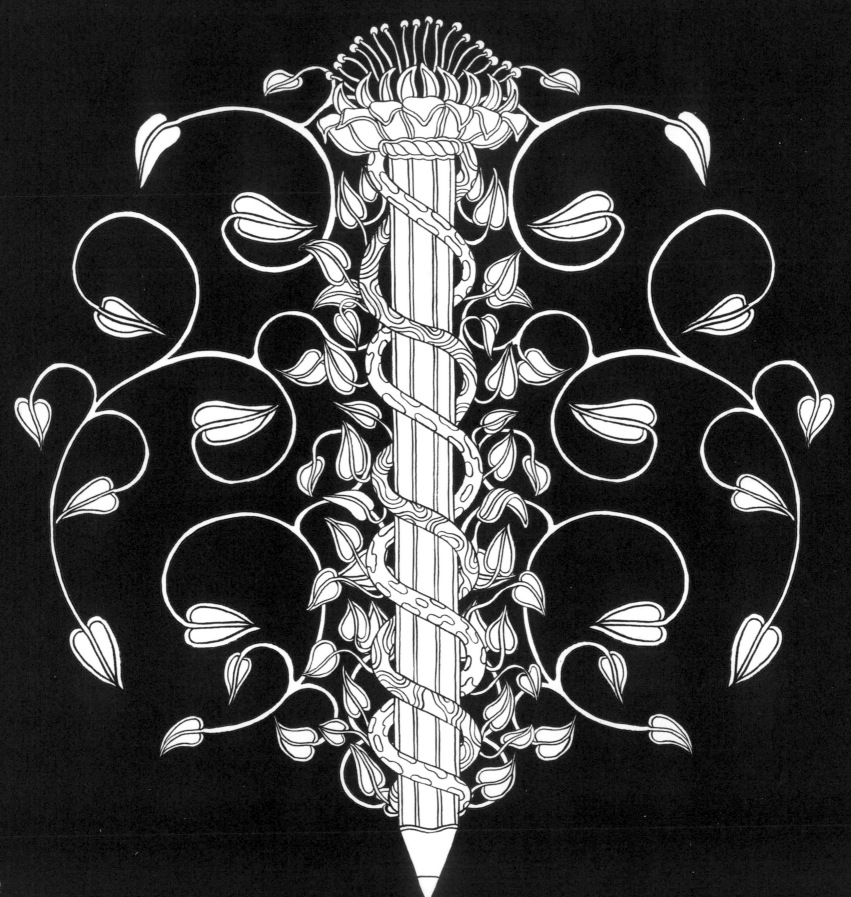

Use the magical PENCIL to guide you through the maze to reach the secret door that leads you out of Wonderland. Please come back soon!

Fairies in Wonderland

Text and illustrations © 2016 by Marcos Chin

HarperCollins books may be purchased for educational, business,
or sales promotional use. For information please e-mail the
Special Markets Department at SPsales@harpercollins.com.

First published in 2016 by
Harper Design
An Imprint of HarperCollins*Publishers*
195 Broadway
New York, NY 10007
Tel: (212) 207-7000
Fax: (855) 746-6023
harperdesign@harpercollins.com
www.hc.com

Distributed throughout the world by
HarperCollins*Publishers*
195 Broadway
New York, NY 10007

ISBN 978-0-06-241998-9

Library of Congress Control Number: 2015936473

Printed in the USA

20 21 PC / LSCW 10 9 8 7 6 5

About the Illustrator

Marcos Chin is an award-winning illustrator whose work has appeared on book and CD covers, in advertisements, fashion catalogs, and magazines. He has worked with MTA Arts for Transit, Neiman Marcus, Fiat, Budweiser, *Time*, *Rolling Stone*, *The New Yorker*, *GQ*, *Sports Illustrated*, and the *New York Times*, and he created the illustrations for the children's book *Ella* by Mallory Kasdan. In 2013 his illustration "Grand Central Catwalk" appeared in New York City subways, celebrating Grand Central Terminal's centennial year. Chin also has a custom design T-shirt label, YEE YEE, which is manufactured in Brooklyn, New York. Chin lectures and gives workshops on illustration throughout the United States and abroad, and also teaches at the School of Visual Arts in New York City. He lives in Brooklyn, New York. **www.marcoschin.com**